Strawberry Shortcake™

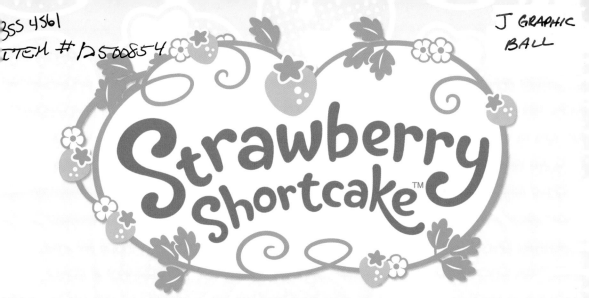

Volume 2:
The Baby Berrykin Baking Challenge Part 2

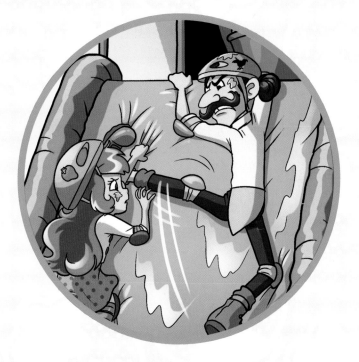

Written by: Georgia Ball
Art by: Amy Mebberson
Colors by: Fernando Peniche
Letters by: Robbie Robbins

ABDO Spotlight
IDW

ABDOPUBLISHING.COM

Reinforced library bound edition published in 2018 by Spotlight, a division of ABDO
PO Box 398166, Minneapolis, Minnesota 55439. Spotlight produces high-quality
reinforced library bound editions for schools and libraries.
Published by agreement with IDW.

Printed in the United States of America, North Mankato, Minnesota.
042017
092017

 THIS BOOK CONTAINS
RECYCLED MATERIALS

PUBLISHER'S CATALOGING IN PUBLICATION DATA

Names: Ball, Georgia, author. | Mebberson, Amy, illustrator.
Title: The baby berrykin baking challenge / writer: Georgia Ball ; art: Amy Mebberson.
Description: Reinforced library bound edition. | Minneapolis, Minnesota : Spotlight, 2018. | Series:
    Strawberry shortcake
Summary: Strawberry Shortcake enters a regional baking competition, but the Purple Piemanne has
    tricks up his sleeves planned to put himself on top.
Identifiers: LCCN 2016961950 | ISBN 9781532140297 (vol. 1, part 1, lib. bdg.) | ISBN
    9781532140303 (vol 2., part 2, lib. bdg.)
Subjects: LCSH: Strawberry Shortcake (Fictitious character)--Juvenile fiction. | Friendship--Juvenile
    fiction. | Comic book, strips, etc.--Juvenile fiction. | Graphic novels--Juvenile fiction.
Classification: DDC 741.5--dc23
LC record available at https://lccn.loc.gov/2016961950

Spotlight

A Division of ABDO
abdopublishing.com

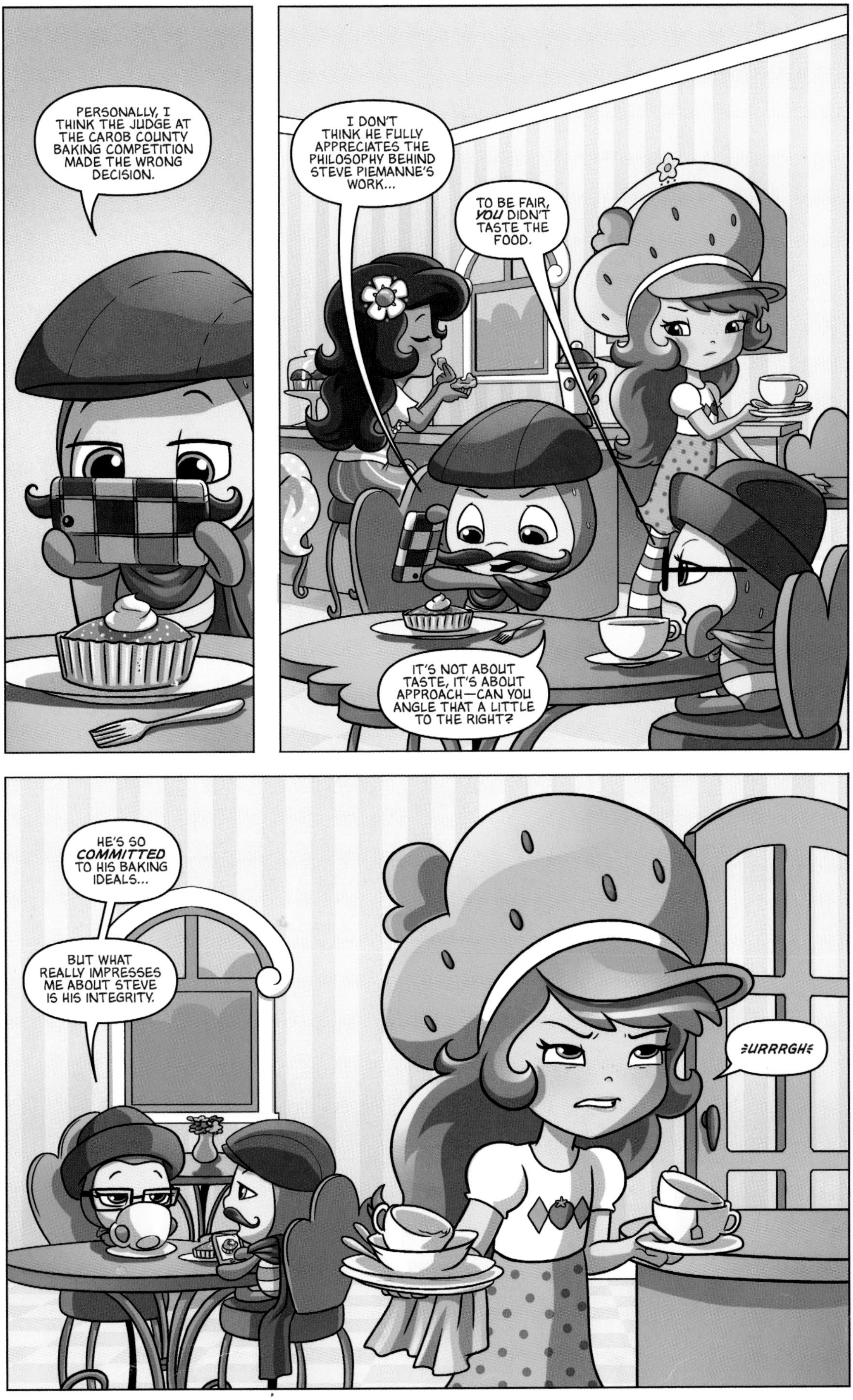
PERSONALLY, I THINK THE JUDGE AT THE CAROB COUNTY BAKING COMPETITION MADE THE WRONG DECISION.
I DON'T THINK HE FULLY APPRECIATES THE PHILOSOPHY BEHIND STEVE PIEMANNE'S WORK...
TO BE FAIR, *YOU* DIDN'T TASTE THE FOOD.
IT'S NOT ABOUT TASTE, IT'S ABOUT APPROACH—CAN YOU ANGLE THAT A LITTLE TO THE RIGHT?
HE'S SO *COMMITTED* TO HIS BAKING IDEALS...
BUT WHAT REALLY IMPRESSES ME ABOUT STEVE IS HIS INTEGRITY.
URRRGH

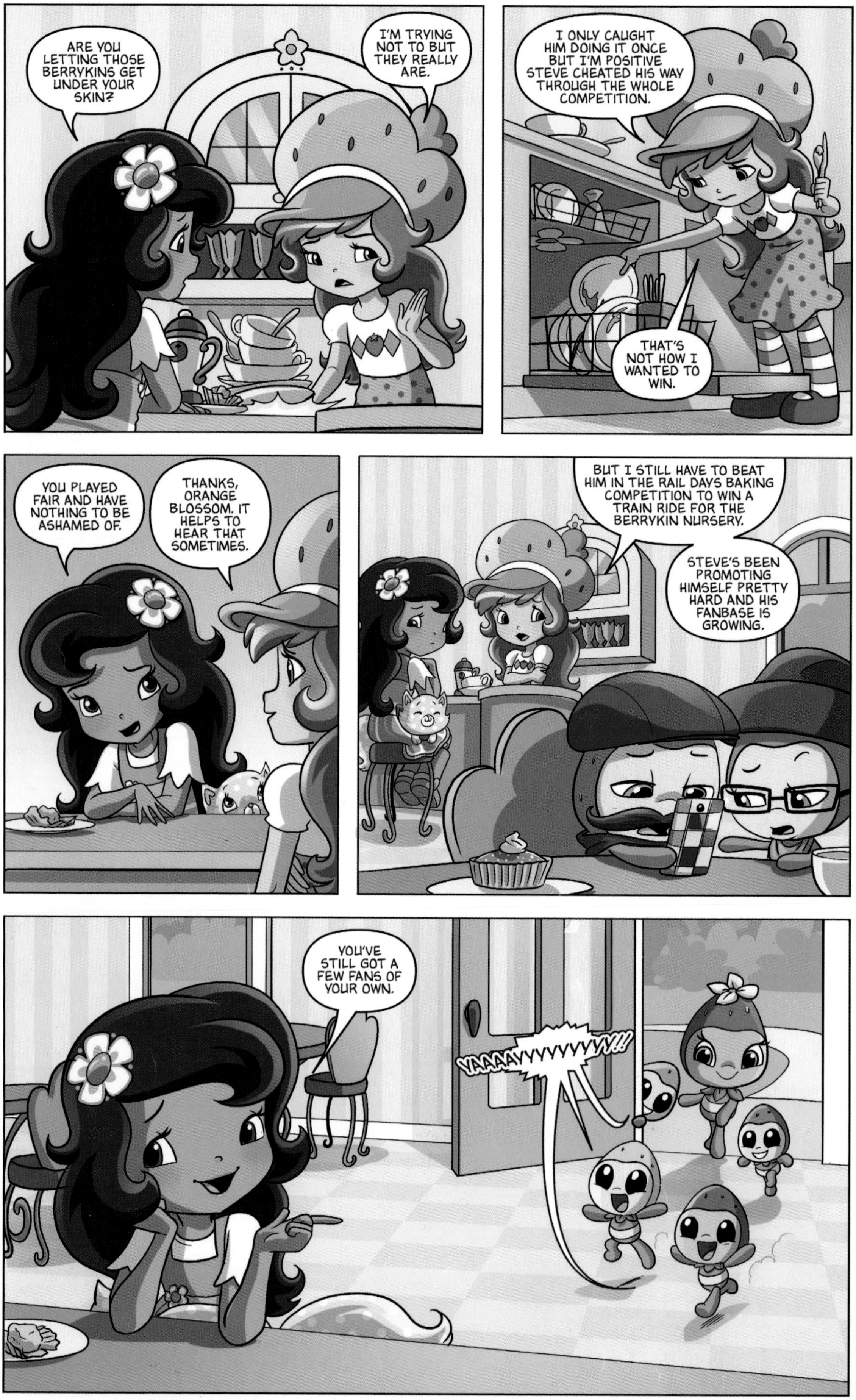
ARE YOU LETTING THOSE BERRYKINS GET UNDER YOUR SKIN?
I'M TRYING NOT TO BUT THEY REALLY ARE.
I ONLY CAUGHT HIM DOING IT ONCE BUT I'M POSITIVE STEVE CHEATED HIS WAY THROUGH THE WHOLE COMPETITION.
THAT'S NOT HOW I WANTED TO WIN.
YOU PLAYED FAIR AND HAVE NOTHING TO BE ASHAMED OF.
THANKS, ORANGE BLOSSOM. IT HELPS TO HEAR THAT SOMETIMES.
BUT I STILL HAVE TO BEAT HIM IN THE RAIL DAYS BAKING COMPETITION TO WIN A TRAIN RIDE FOR THE BERRYKIN NURSERY.
STEVE'S BEEN PROMOTING HIMSELF PRETTY HARD AND HIS FANBASE IS GROWING.
YOU'VE STILL GOT A FEW FANS OF YOUR OWN.
YAAAAYYYYYYYYY!!

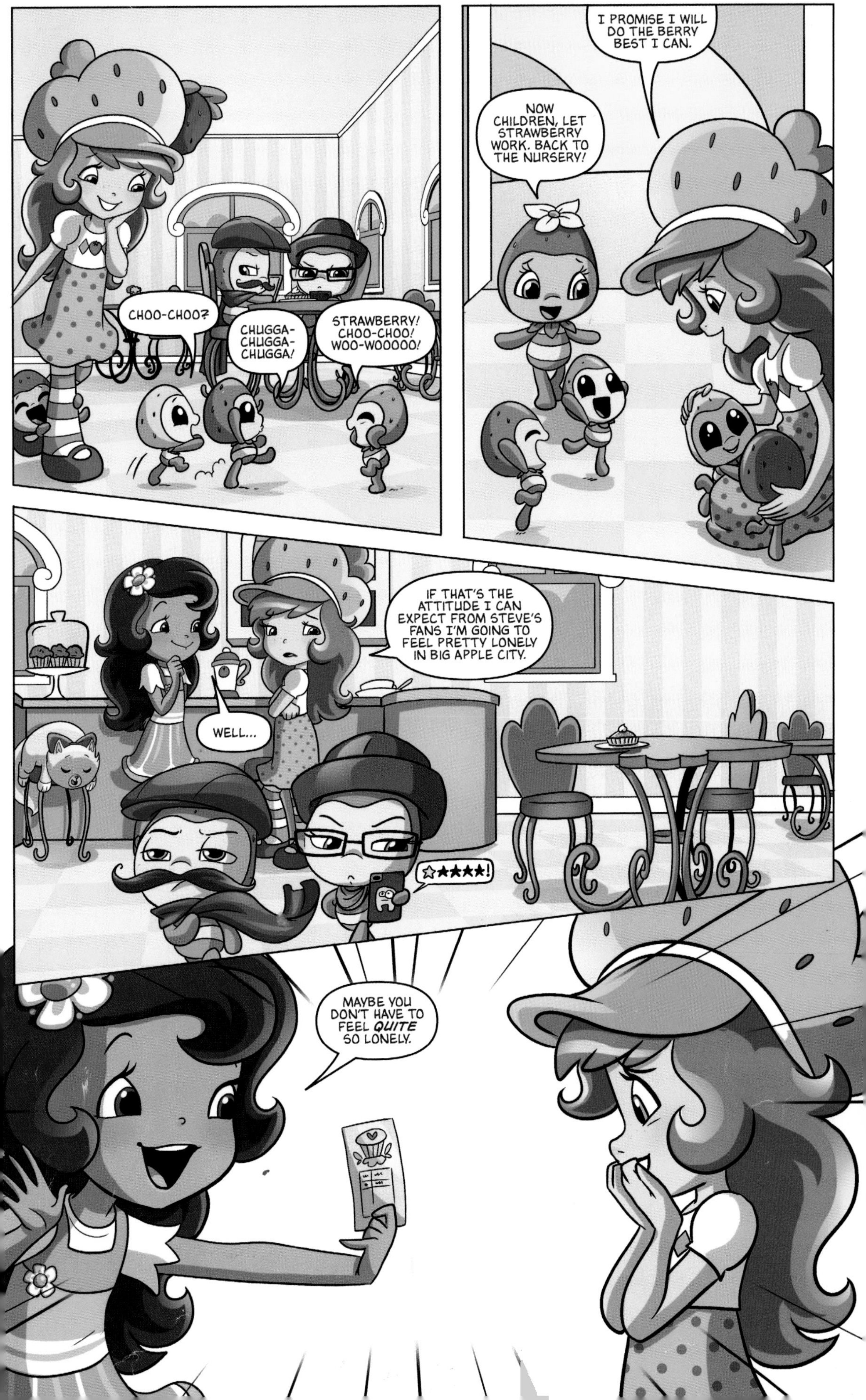
CHOO-CHOO?
CHUGGA-CHUGGA-CHUGGA!
STRAWBERRY! CHOO-CHOO! WOO-WOOOOO!
NOW CHILDREN, LET STRAWBERRY WORK. BACK TO THE NURSERY!
I PROMISE I WILL DO THE BERRY BEST I CAN.
IF THAT'S THE ATTITUDE I CAN EXPECT FROM STEVE'S FANS I'M GOING TO FEEL PRETTY LONELY IN BIG APPLE CITY.
WELL...
☆★★★★!
MAYBE YOU DON'T HAVE TO FEEL *QUITE* SO LONELY.

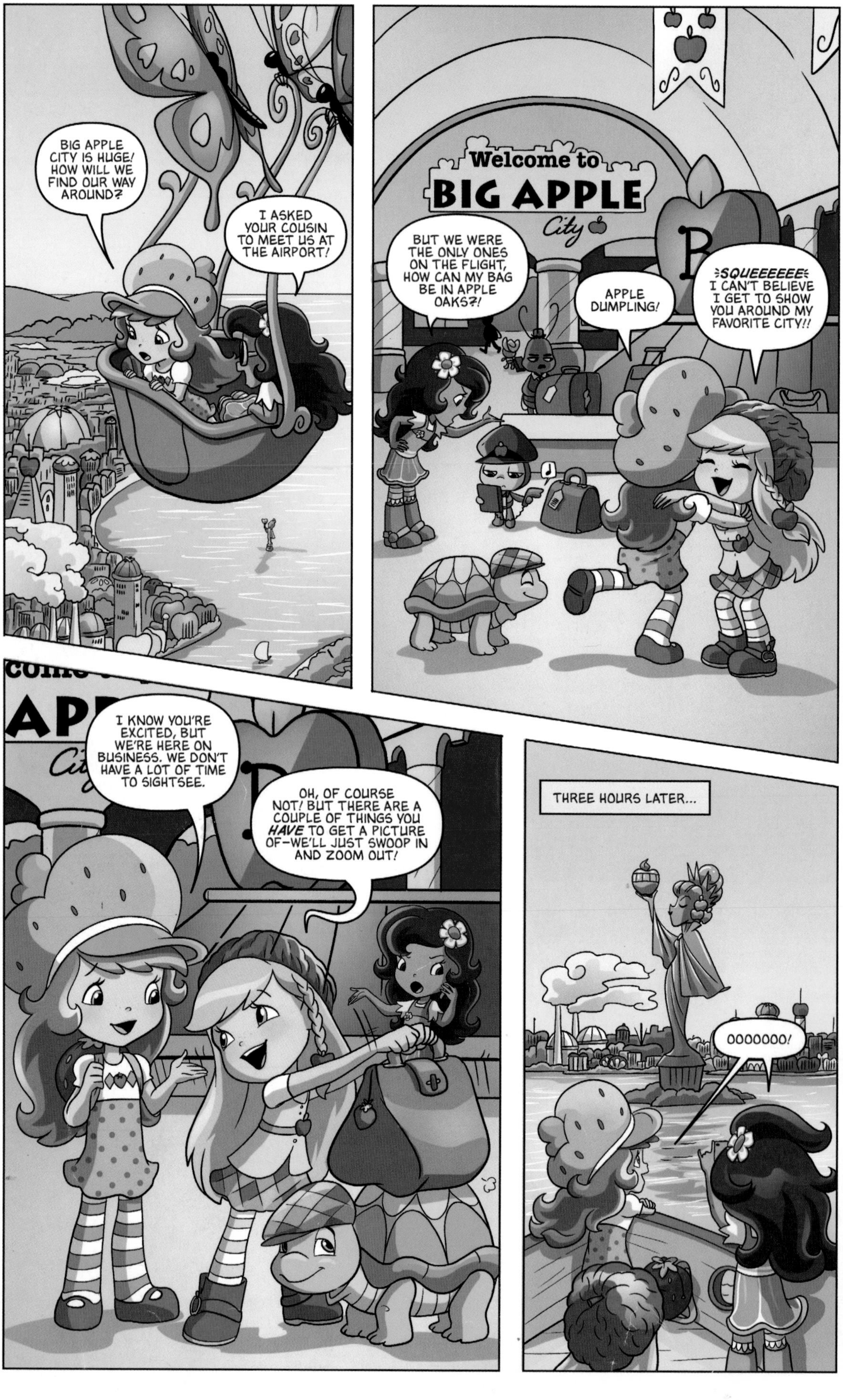
BIG APPLE CITY IS HUGE! HOW WILL WE FIND OUR WAY AROUND?
I ASKED YOUR COUSIN TO MEET US AT THE AIRPORT!
Welcome to BIG APPLE City
BUT WE WERE THE ONLY ONES ON THE FLIGHT, HOW CAN MY BAG BE IN APPLE OAKS?!
APPLE DUMPLING!
SQUEEEEEE I CAN'T BELIEVE I GET TO SHOW YOU AROUND MY FAVORITE CITY!!
I KNOW YOU'RE EXCITED, BUT WE'RE HERE ON BUSINESS. WE DON'T HAVE A LOT OF TIME TO SIGHTSEE.
OH, OF COURSE NOT! BUT THERE ARE A COUPLE OF THINGS YOU *HAVE* TO GET A PICTURE OF—WE'LL JUST SWOOP IN AND ZOOM OUT!
THREE HOURS LATER...
OOOOOOO!

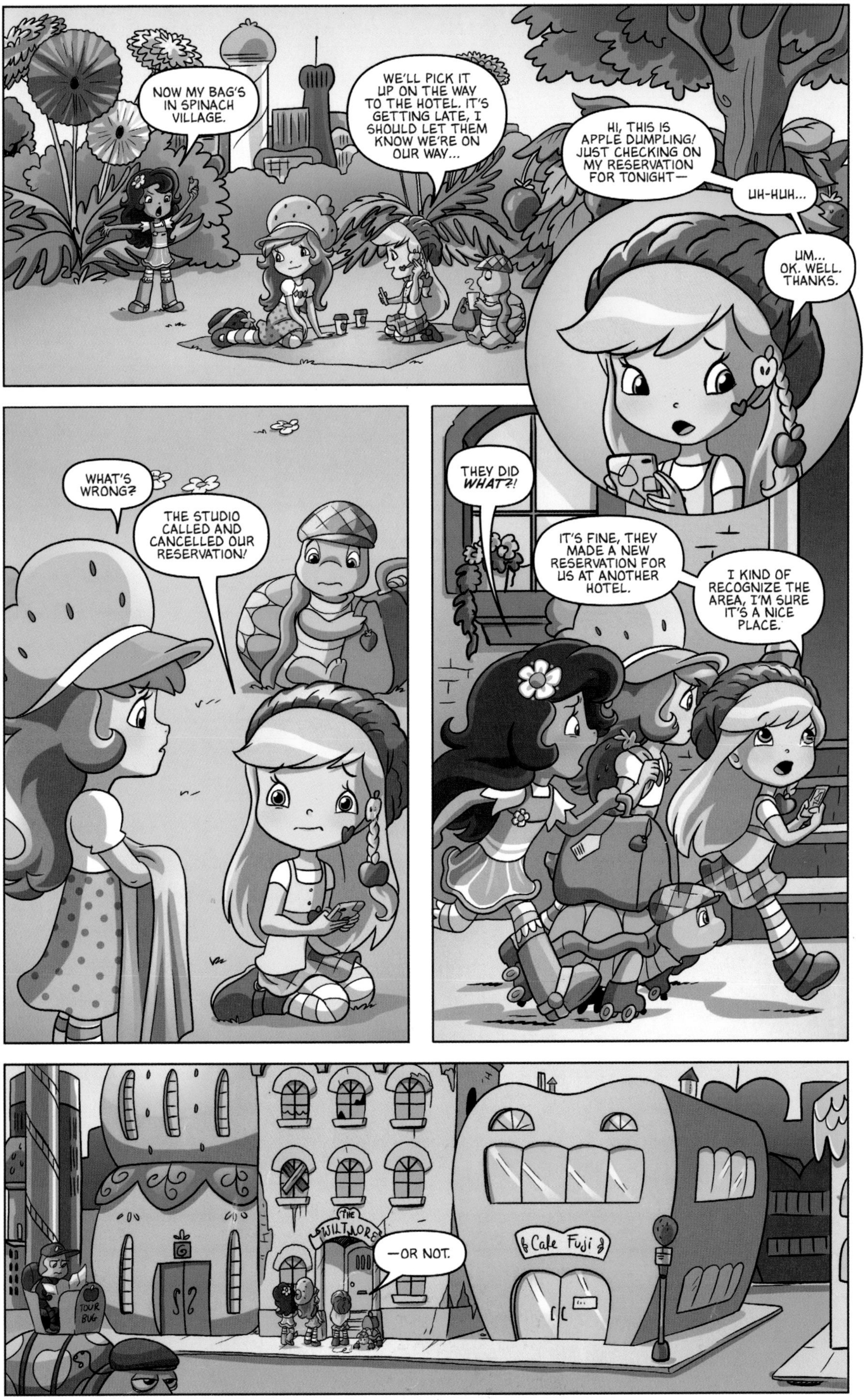
NOW MY BAG'S IN SPINACH VILLAGE.
WE'LL PICK IT UP ON THE WAY TO THE HOTEL. IT'S GETTING LATE, I SHOULD LET THEM KNOW WE'RE ON OUR WAY...
HI, THIS IS APPLE DUMPLING! JUST CHECKING ON MY RESERVATION FOR TONIGHT—
UH-HUH...
UM... OK. WELL. THANKS.
WHAT'S WRONG?
THE STUDIO CALLED AND CANCELLED OUR RESERVATION!
THEY DID *WHAT?!*
IT'S FINE, THEY MADE A NEW RESERVATION FOR US AT ANOTHER HOTEL.
I KIND OF RECOGNIZE THE AREA, I'M SURE IT'S A NICE PLACE.
THE WILTMORE
—OR NOT.
TOUR BUG
Cafe Fuji

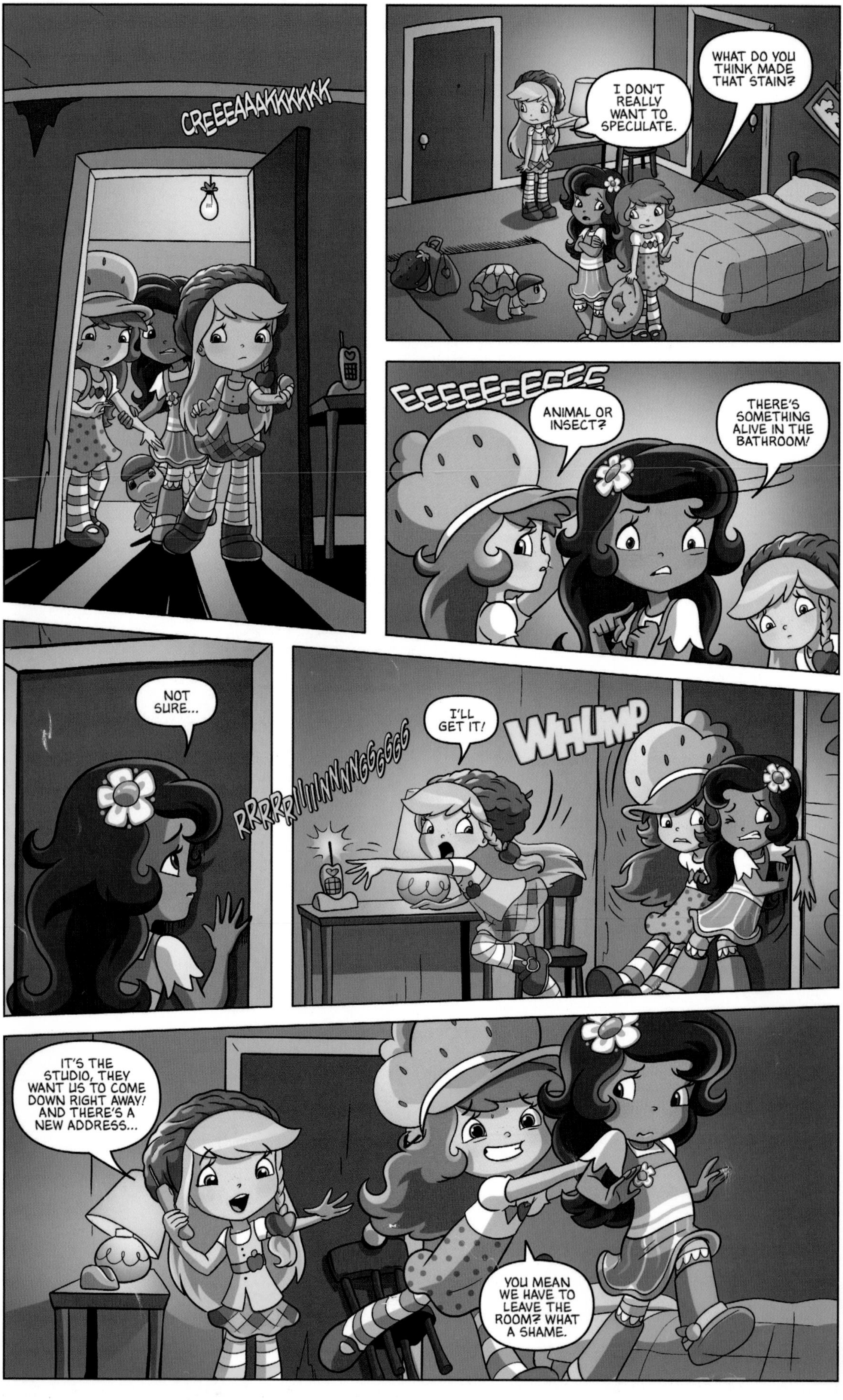
CREEEAAAKKKKKK
I DON'T REALLY WANT TO SPECULATE.
WHAT DO YOU THINK MADE THAT STAIN?
EEEEEEEEEEE
ANIMAL OR INSECT?
THERE'S SOMETHING ALIVE IN THE BATHROOM!
NOT SURE...
RRRRRIIIINNNNGGGGG
I'LL GET IT!
WHUMP
IT'S THE STUDIO, THEY WANT US TO COME DOWN RIGHT AWAY! AND THERE'S A NEW ADDRESS...
YOU MEAN WE HAVE TO LEAVE THE ROOM? WHAT A SHAME.

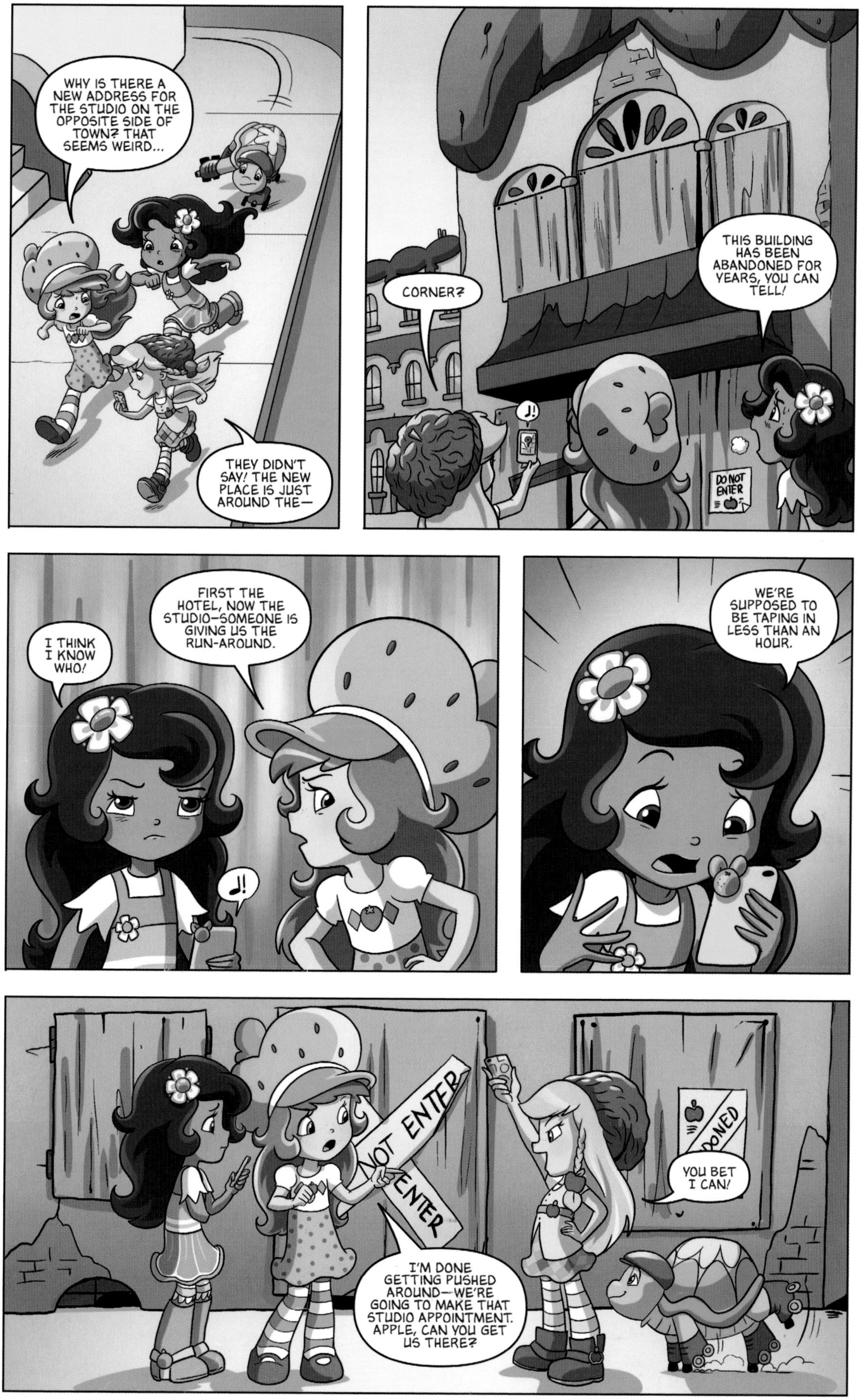
WHY IS THERE A NEW ADDRESS FOR THE STUDIO ON THE OPPOSITE SIDE OF TOWN? THAT SEEMS WEIRD...
THEY DIDN'T SAY! THE NEW PLACE IS JUST AROUND THE—
CORNER?
THIS BUILDING HAS BEEN ABANDONED FOR YEARS, YOU CAN TELL!
DO NOT ENTER
FIRST THE HOTEL, NOW THE STUDIO—SOMEONE IS GIVING US THE RUN-AROUND.
I THINK I KNOW WHO!
WE'RE SUPPOSED TO BE TAPING IN LESS THAN AN HOUR.
I'M DONE GETTING PUSHED AROUND—WE'RE GOING TO MAKE THAT STUDIO APPOINTMENT. APPLE, CAN YOU GET US THERE?
YOU BET I CAN!

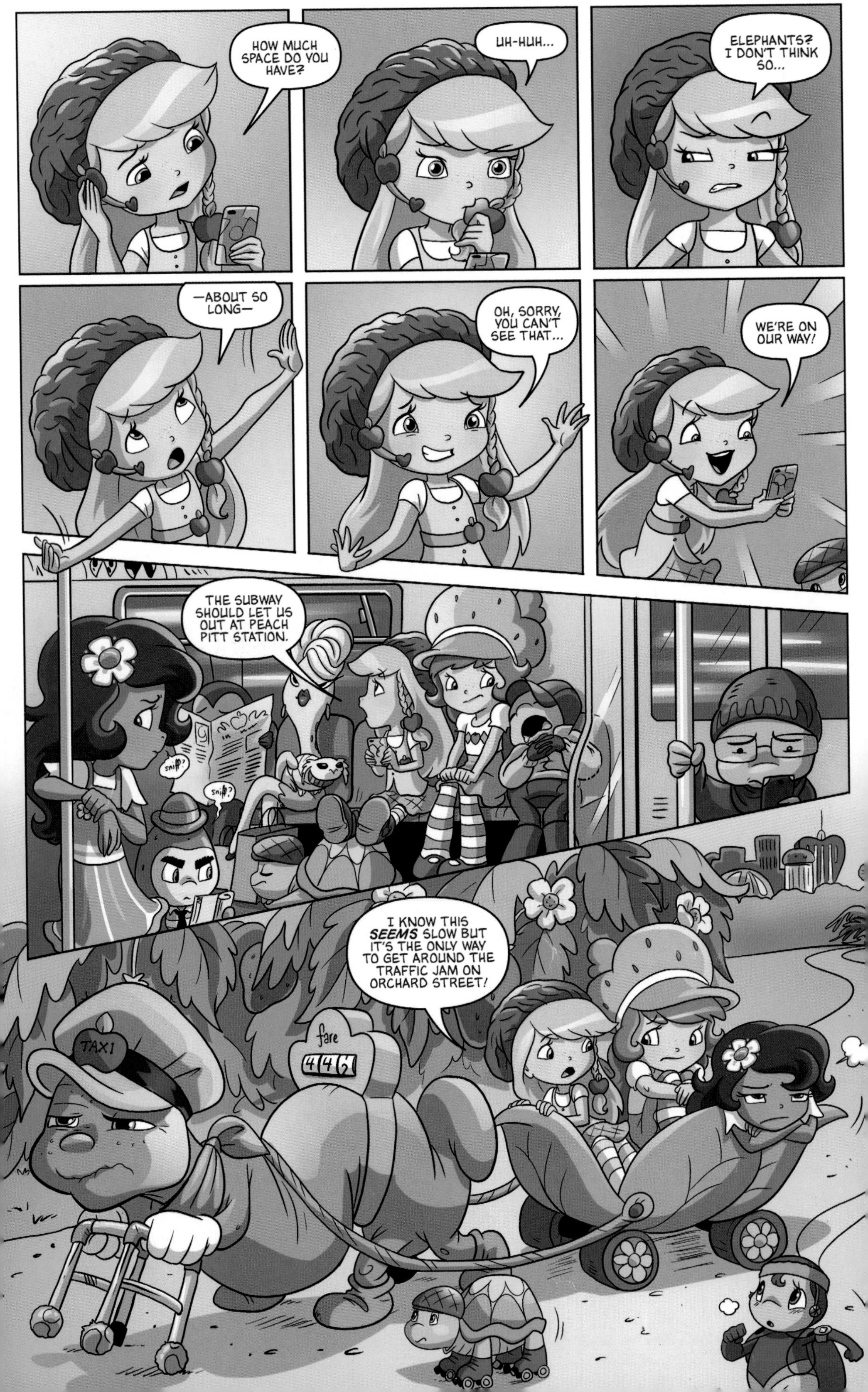
HOW MUCH SPACE DO YOU HAVE?
UH-HUH...
ELEPHANTS? I DON'T THINK SO...
—ABOUT SO LONG—
OH, SORRY, YOU CAN'T SEE THAT...
WE'RE ON OUR WAY!
THE SUBWAY SHOULD LET US OUT AT PEACH PITT STATION.
sniff?
sniff?
I KNOW THIS SEEMS SLOW BUT IT'S THE ONLY WAY TO GET AROUND THE TRAFFIC JAM ON ORCHARD STREET!
TAXI
fare
446

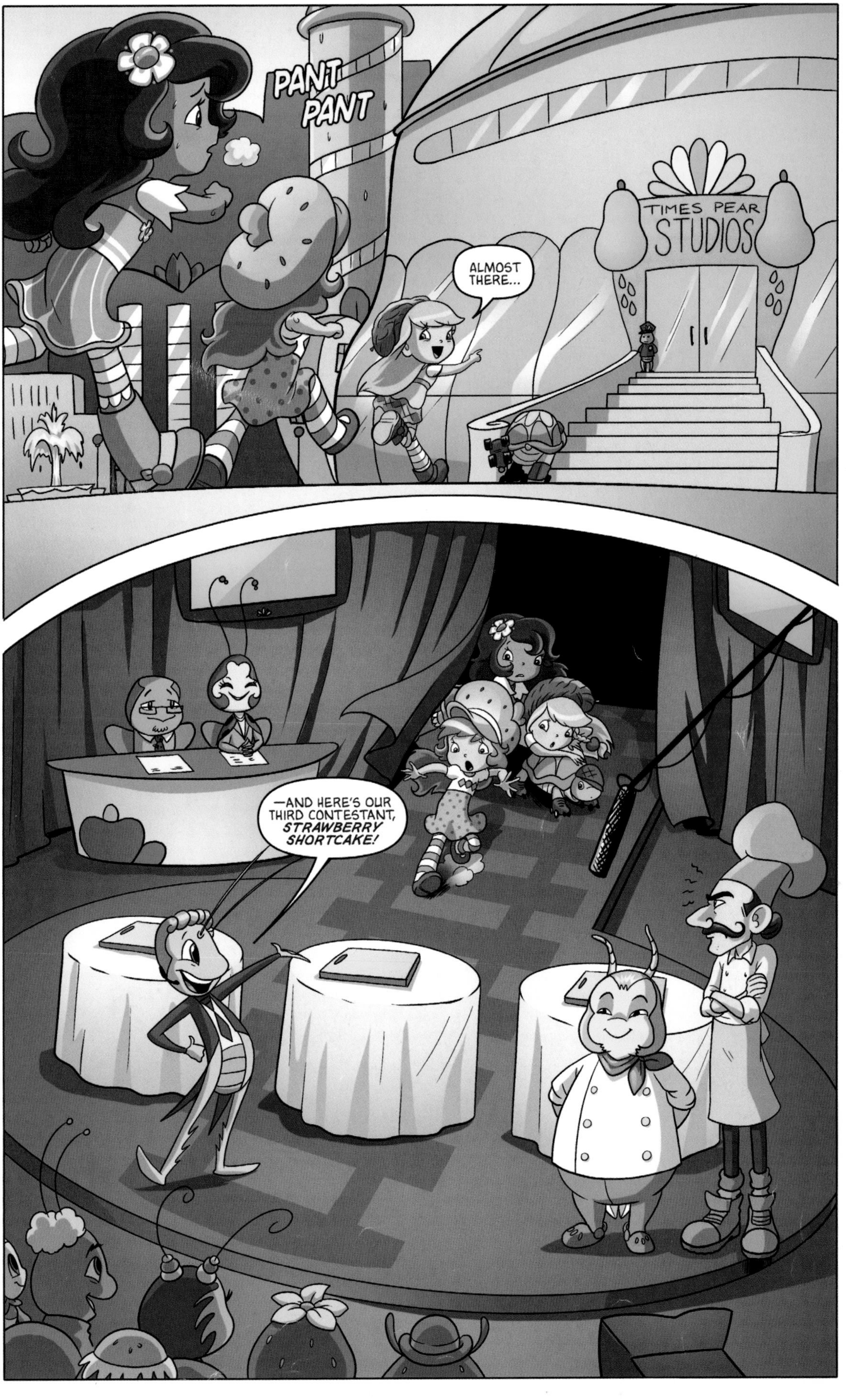
PANT PANT
ALMOST THERE...
TIMES PEAR STUDIOS
—AND HERE'S OUR THIRD CONTESTANT, *STRAWBERRY SHORTCAKE!*

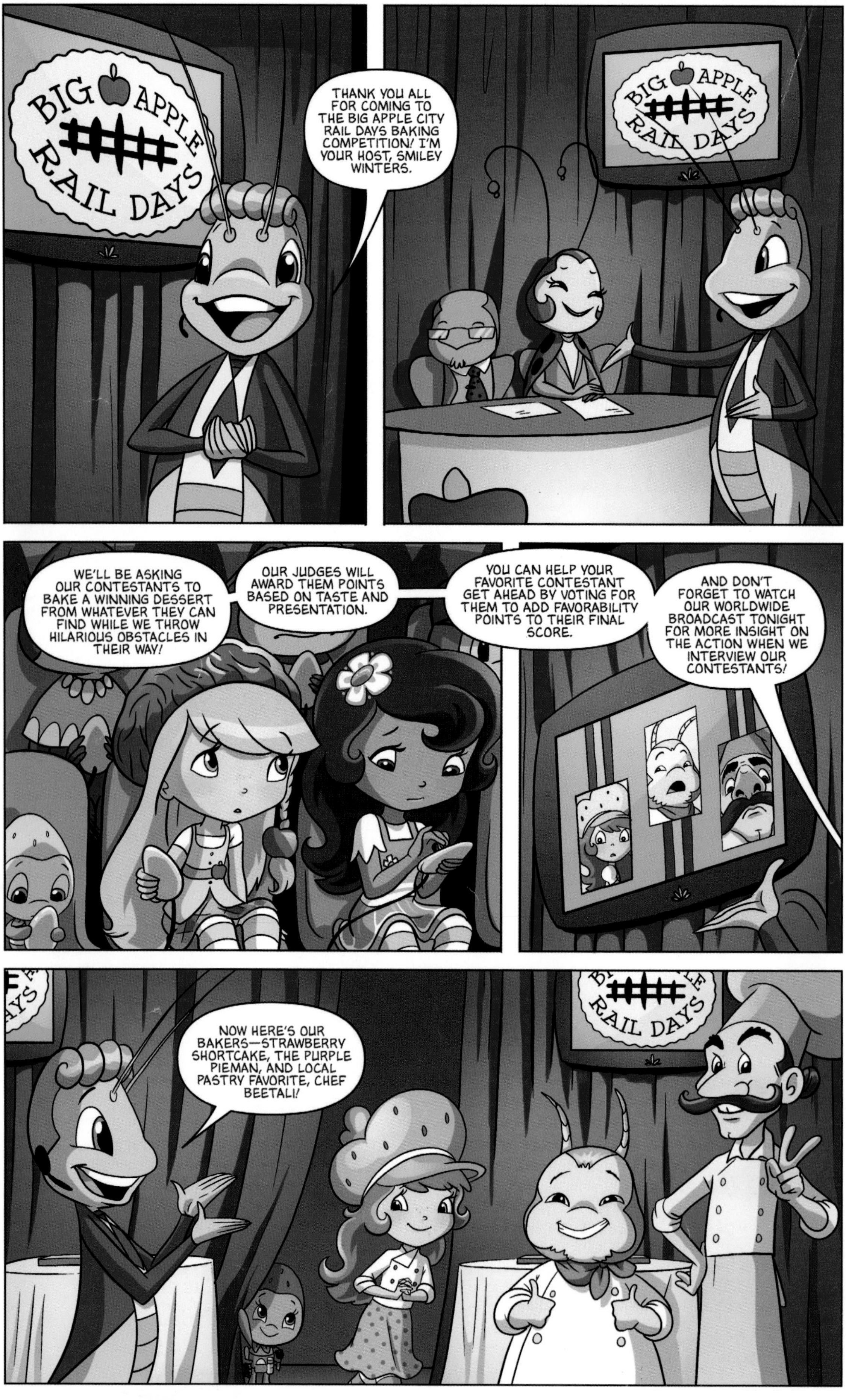
BIG APPLE RAIL DAYS
THANK YOU ALL FOR COMING TO THE BIG APPLE CITY RAIL DAYS BAKING COMPETITION! I'M YOUR HOST, SMILEY WINTERS.
BIG APPLE RAIL DAYS
WE'LL BE ASKING OUR CONTESTANTS TO BAKE A WINNING DESSERT FROM WHATEVER THEY CAN FIND WHILE WE THROW HILARIOUS OBSTACLES IN THEIR WAY!
OUR JUDGES WILL AWARD THEM POINTS BASED ON TASTE AND PRESENTATION.
YOU CAN HELP YOUR FAVORITE CONTESTANT GET AHEAD BY VOTING FOR THEM TO ADD FAVORABILITY POINTS TO THEIR FINAL SCORE.
AND DON'T FORGET TO WATCH OUR WORLDWIDE BROADCAST TONIGHT FOR MORE INSIGHT ON THE ACTION WHEN WE INTERVIEW OUR CONTESTANTS!
RAIL DAYS
NOW HERE'S OUR BAKERS—STRAWBERRY SHORTCAKE, THE PURPLE PIEMAN, AND LOCAL PASTRY FAVORITE, CHEF BEETALI!

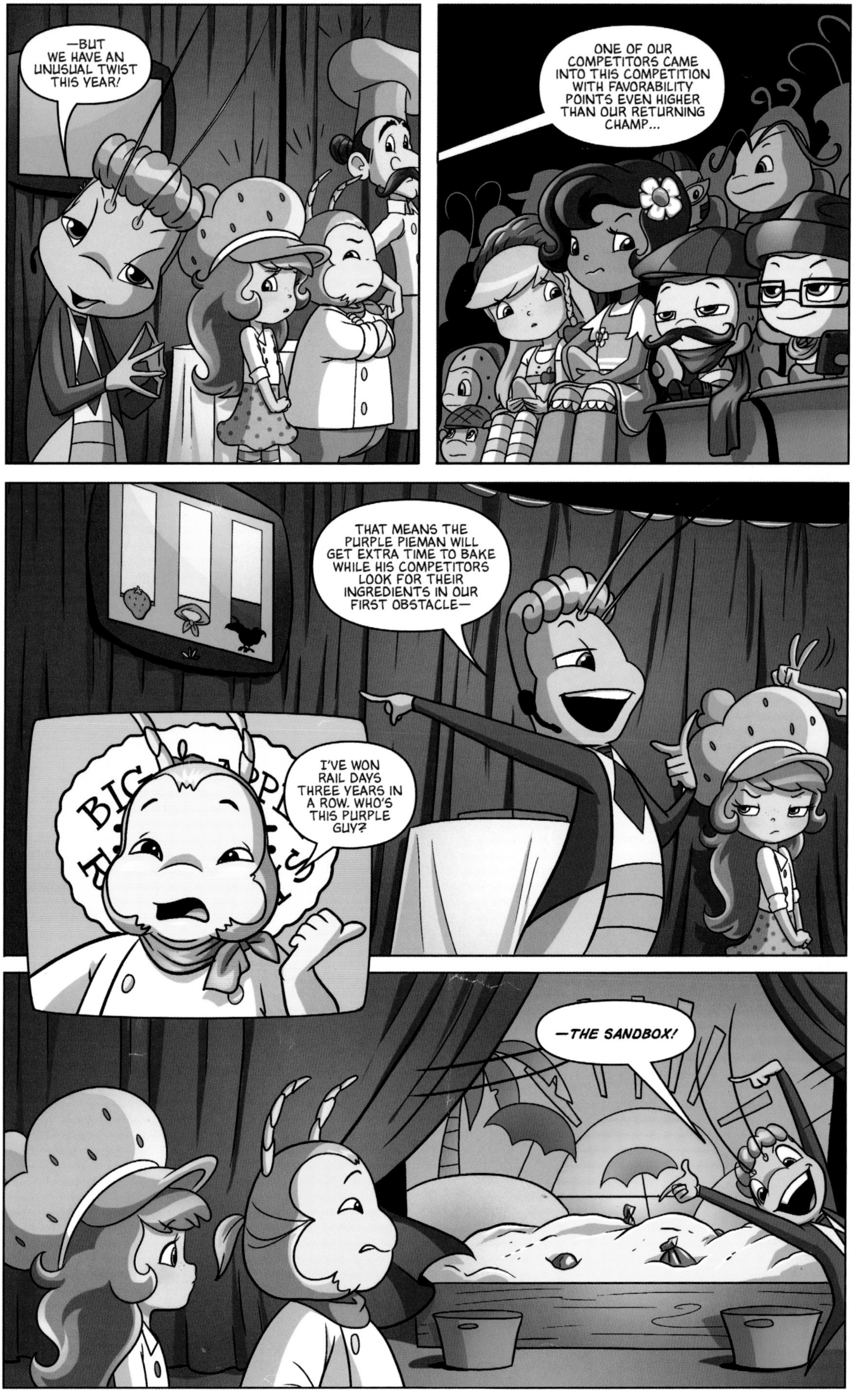
—BUT WE HAVE AN UNUSUAL TWIST THIS YEAR!
ONE OF OUR COMPETITORS CAME INTO THIS COMPETITION WITH FAVORABILITY POINTS EVEN HIGHER THAN OUR RETURNING CHAMP...
THAT MEANS THE PURPLE PIEMAN WILL GET EXTRA TIME TO BAKE WHILE HIS COMPETITORS LOOK FOR THEIR INGREDIENTS IN OUR FIRST OBSTACLE—
I'VE WON RAIL DAYS THREE YEARS IN A ROW. WHO'S THIS PURPLE GUY?
—THE SANDBOX!

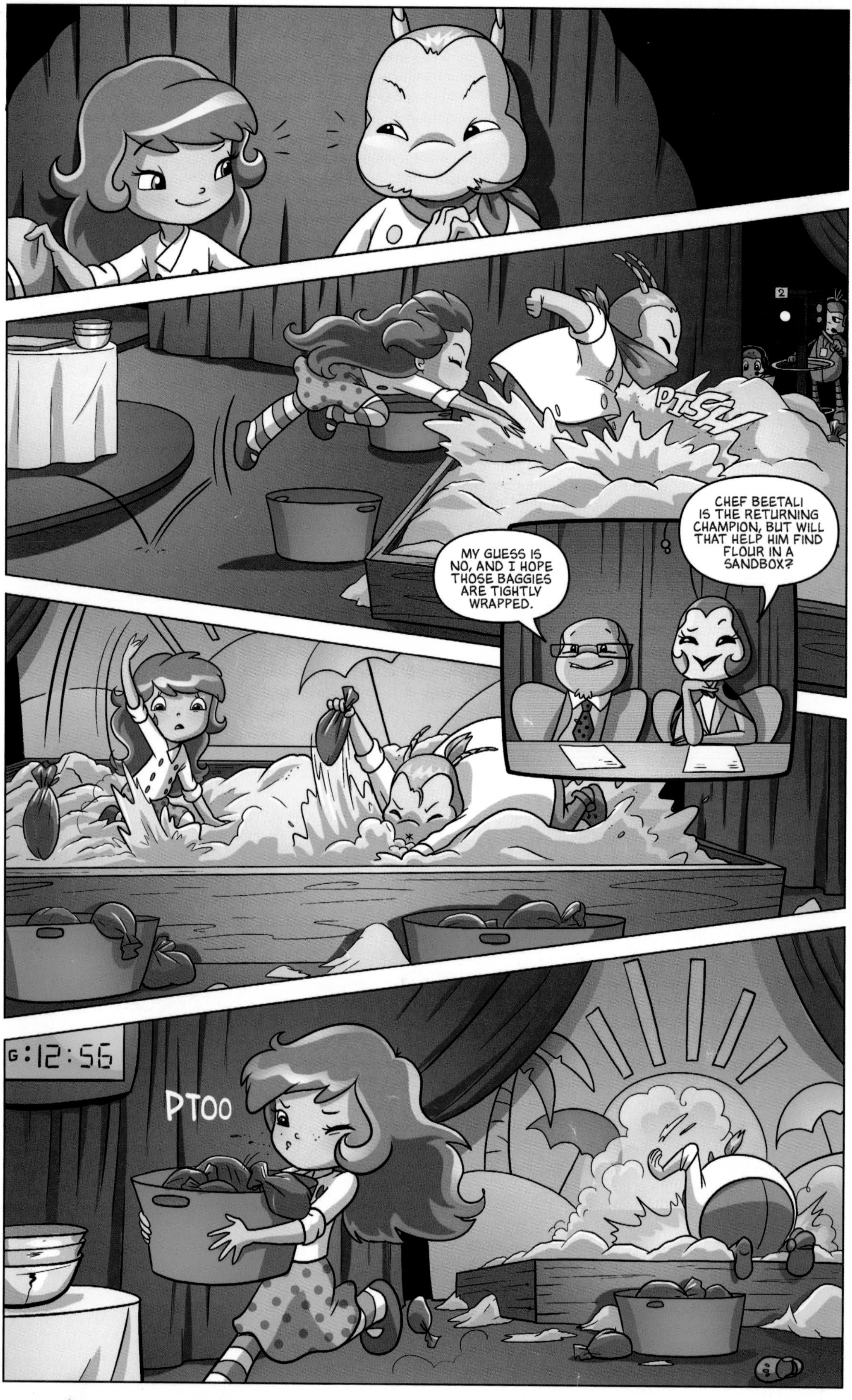
2
PISH
CHEF BEETALI IS THE RETURNING CHAMPION, BUT WILL THAT HELP HIM FIND FLOUR IN A SANDBOX?
MY GUESS IS NO, AND I HOPE THOSE BAGGIES ARE TIGHTLY WRAPPED.
G:12:56
PTOO

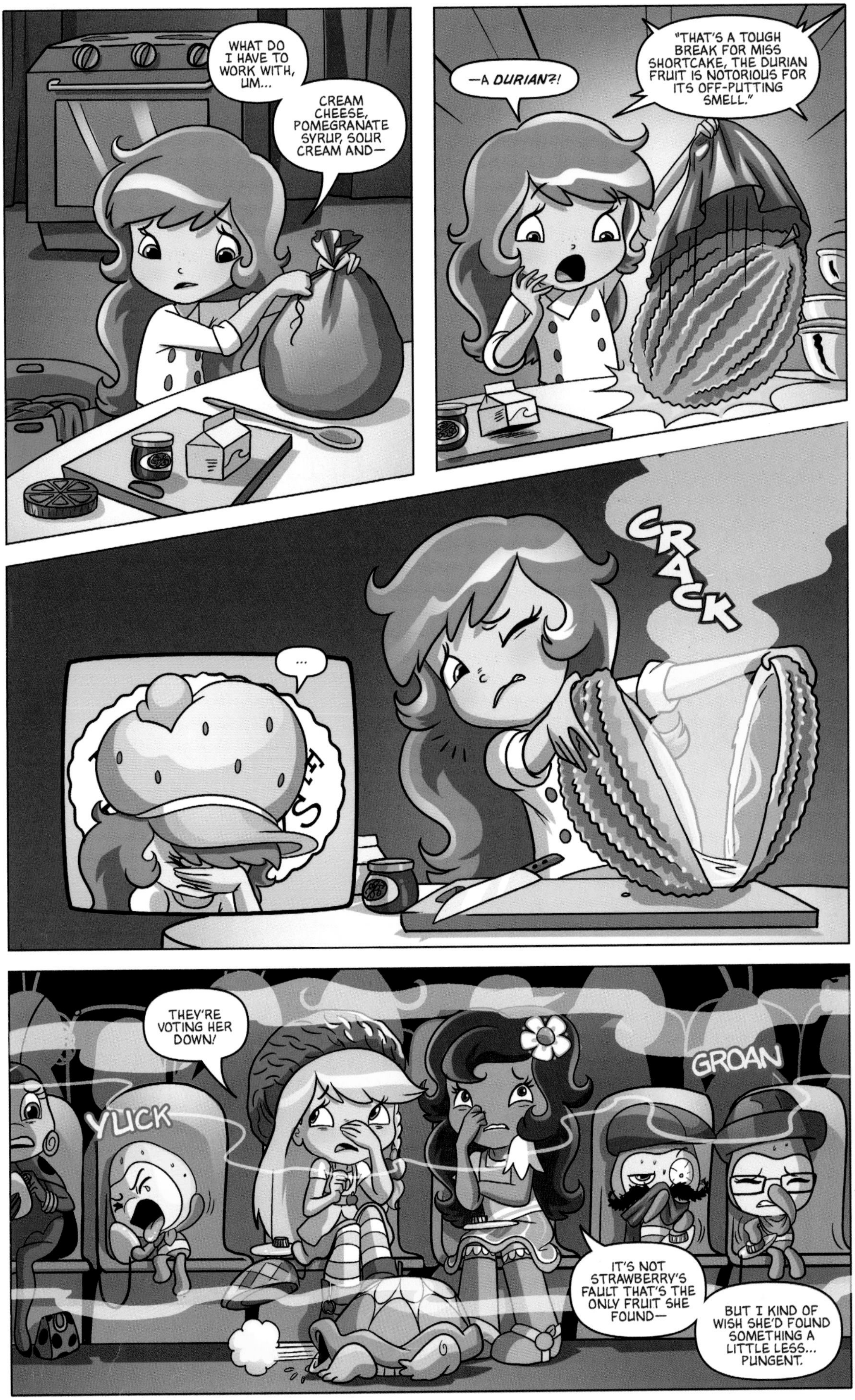
WHAT DO I HAVE TO WORK WITH, UM...
CREAM CHEESE, POMEGRANATE SYRUP, SOUR CREAM AND—
—A *DURIAN*?!
"THAT'S A TOUGH BREAK FOR MISS SHORTCAKE, THE DURIAN FRUIT IS NOTORIOUS FOR ITS OFF-PUTTING SMELL."
CRACK
...
THEY'RE VOTING HER DOWN!
YUCK
GROAN
IT'S NOT STRAWBERRY'S FAULT THAT'S THE ONLY FRUIT SHE FOUND—
BUT I KIND OF WISH SHE'D FOUND SOMETHING A LITTLE LESS... PUNGENT.

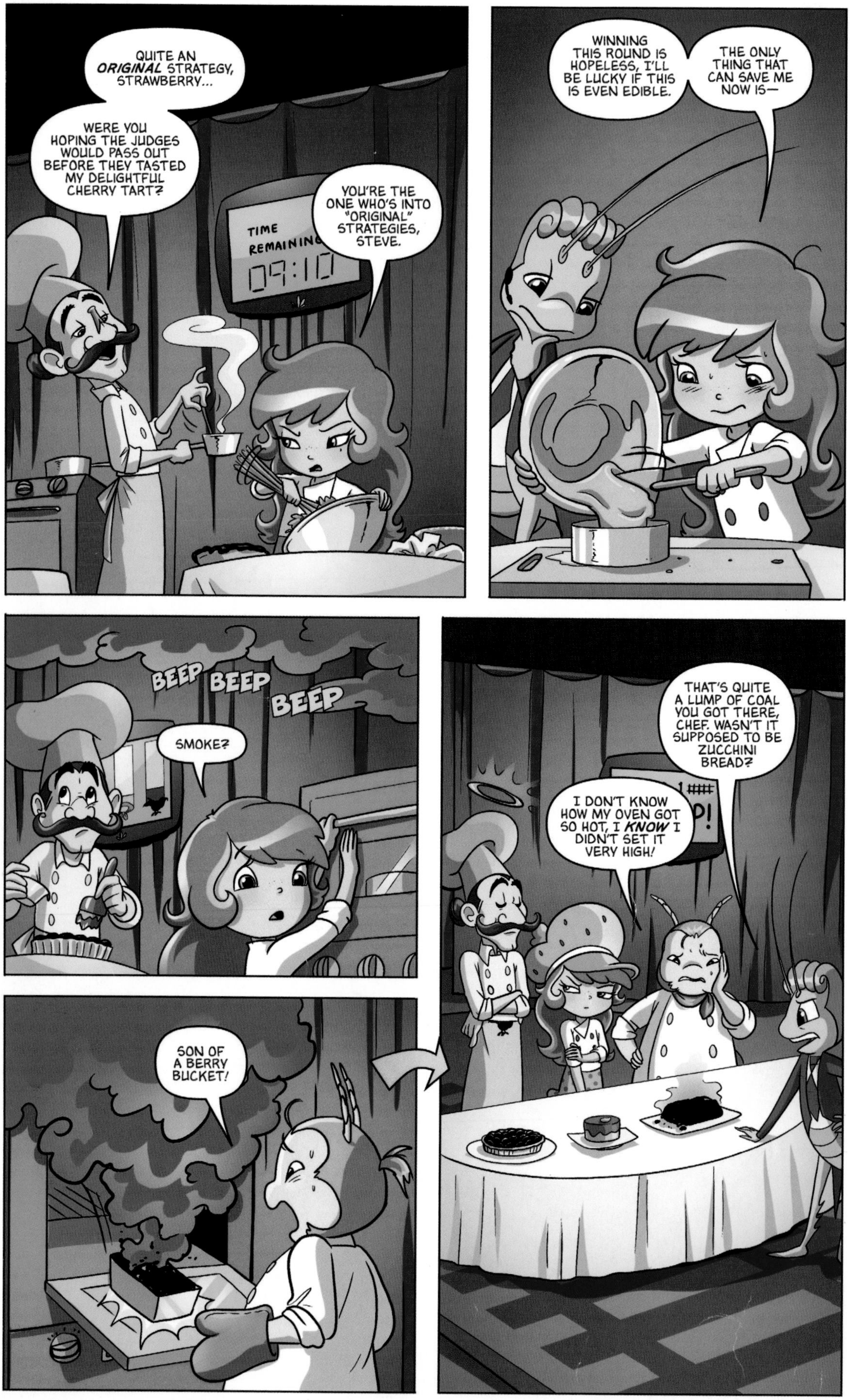
QUITE AN *ORIGINAL* STRATEGY, STRAWBERRY...
WERE YOU HOPING THE JUDGES WOULD PASS OUT BEFORE THEY TASTED MY DELIGHTFUL CHERRY TART?
TIME REMAINING
09:10
YOU'RE THE ONE WHO'S INTO "ORIGINAL" STRATEGIES, STEVE.
WINNING THIS ROUND IS HOPELESS, I'LL BE LUCKY IF THIS IS EVEN EDIBLE.
THE ONLY THING THAT CAN SAVE ME NOW IS—
BEEP BEEP BEEP
SMOKE?
SON OF A BERRY BUCKET!
THAT'S QUITE A LUMP OF COAL YOU GOT THERE, CHEF. WASN'T IT SUPPOSED TO BE ZUCCHINI BREAD?
I DON'T KNOW HOW MY OVEN GOT SO HOT, I *KNOW* I DIDN'T SET IT VERY HIGH!

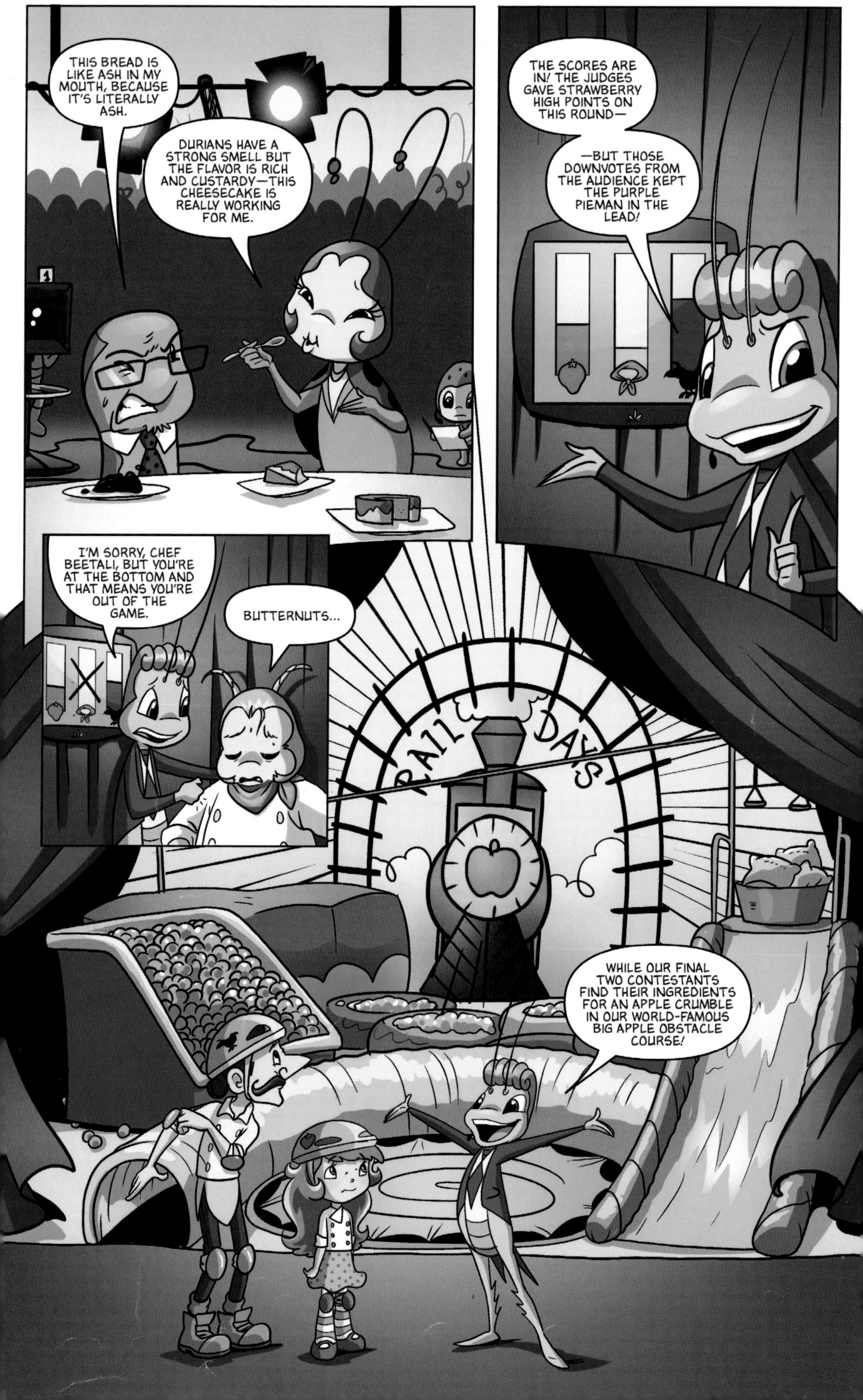
THIS BREAD IS LIKE ASH IN MY MOUTH, BECAUSE IT'S LITERALLY ASH.
DURIANS HAVE A STRONG SMELL BUT THE FLAVOR IS RICH AND CUSTARDY—THIS CHEESECAKE IS REALLY WORKING FOR ME.
THE SCORES ARE IN! THE JUDGES GAVE STRAWBERRY HIGH POINTS ON THIS ROUND—
—BUT THOSE DOWNVOTES FROM THE AUDIENCE KEPT THE PURPLE PIEMAN IN THE LEAD!
I'M SORRY, CHEF BEETALI, BUT YOU'RE AT THE BOTTOM AND THAT MEANS YOU'RE OUT OF THE GAME.
BUTTERNUTS...
RAIL DAYS
WHILE OUR FINAL TWO CONTESTANTS FIND THEIR INGREDIENTS FOR AN APPLE CRUMBLE IN OUR WORLD-FAMOUS BIG APPLE OBSTACLE COURSE!

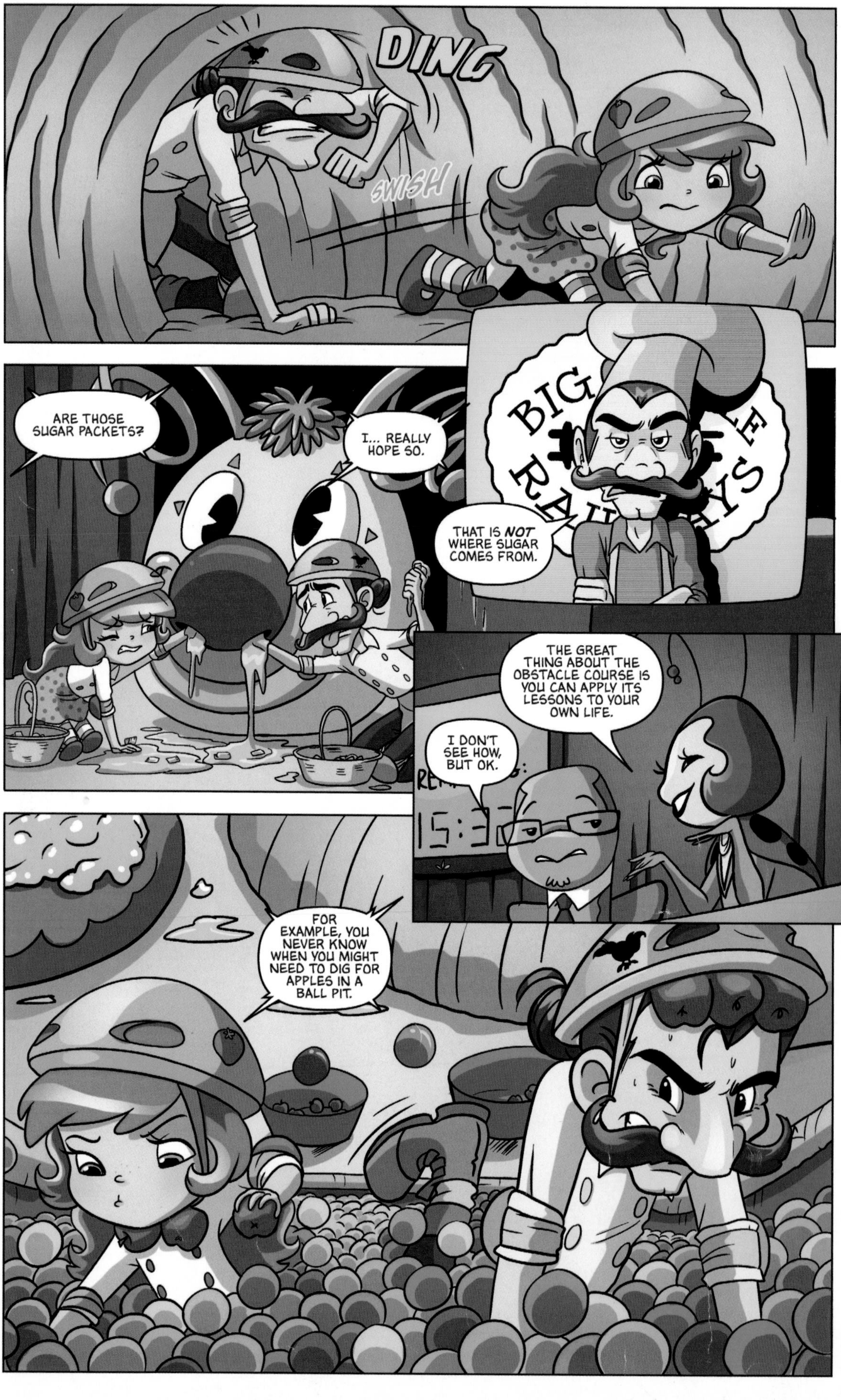
DING
SWISH
ARE THOSE SUGAR PACKETS?
I... REALLY HOPE SO.
THAT IS *NOT* WHERE SUGAR COMES FROM.
THE GREAT THING ABOUT THE OBSTACLE COURSE IS YOU CAN APPLY ITS LESSONS TO YOUR OWN LIFE.
I DON'T SEE HOW, BUT OK.
FOR EXAMPLE, YOU NEVER KNOW WHEN YOU MIGHT NEED TO DIG FOR APPLES IN A BALL PIT.

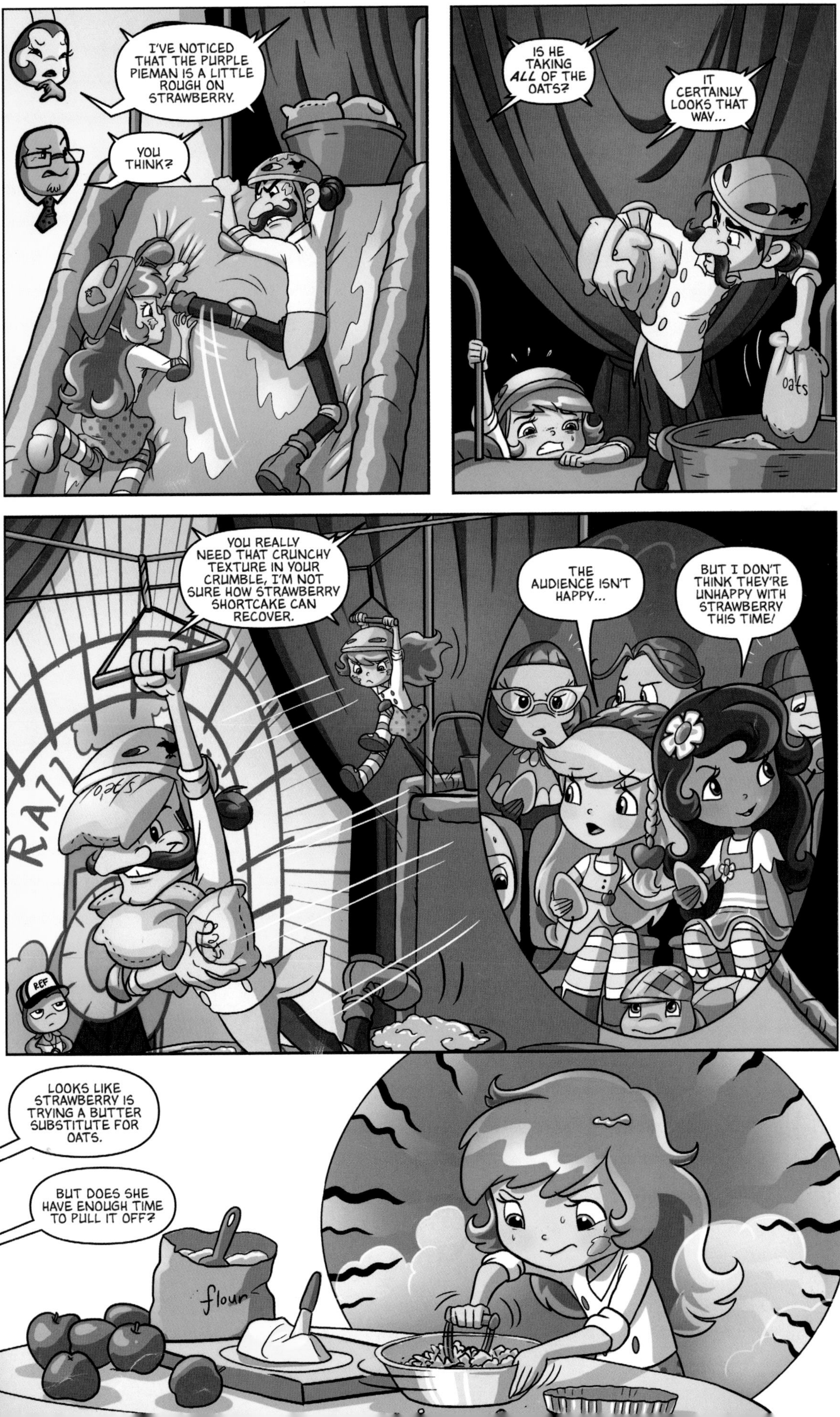
I'VE NOTICED THAT THE PURPLE PIEMAN IS A LITTLE ROUGH ON STRAWBERRY.
YOU THINK?
IS HE TAKING ALL OF THE OATS?
IT CERTAINLY LOOKS THAT WAY...
oats
YOU REALLY NEED THAT CRUNCHY TEXTURE IN YOUR CRUMBLE, I'M NOT SURE HOW STRAWBERRY SHORTCAKE CAN RECOVER.
THE AUDIENCE ISN'T HAPPY...
BUT I DON'T THINK THEY'RE UNHAPPY WITH STRAWBERRY THIS TIME!
REF
LOOKS LIKE STRAWBERRY IS TRYING A BUTTER SUBSTITUTE FOR OATS.
BUT DOES SHE HAVE ENOUGH TIME TO PULL IT OFF?
flour

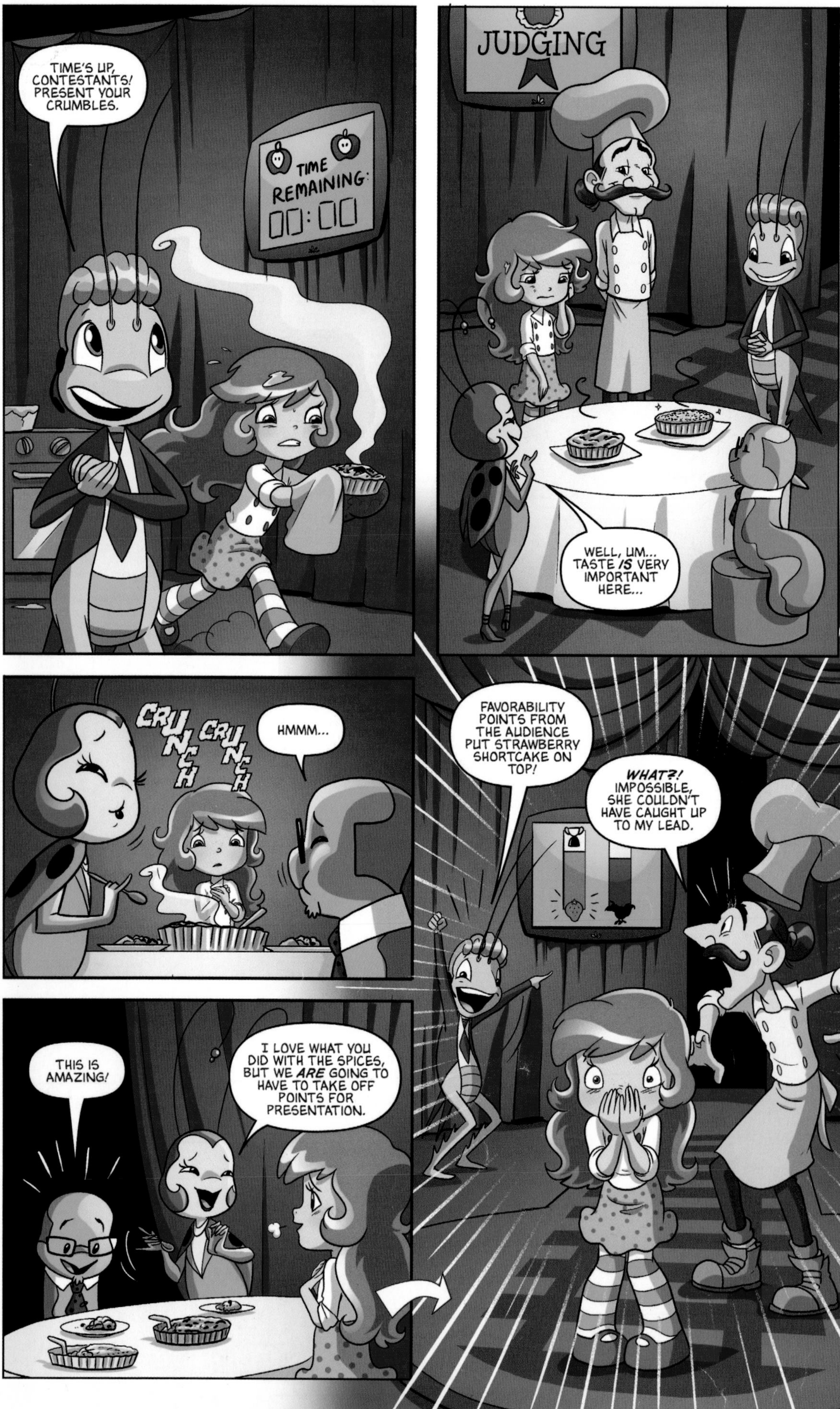
TIME'S UP, CONTESTANTS! PRESENT YOUR CRUMBLES.
TIME REMAINING: 00:00
JUDGING
WELL, UM... TASTE IS VERY IMPORTANT HERE...
CRUNCH CRUNCH
HMMM...
THIS IS AMAZING!
I LOVE WHAT YOU DID WITH THE SPICES, BUT WE ARE GOING TO HAVE TO TAKE OFF POINTS FOR PRESENTATION.
FAVORABILITY POINTS FROM THE AUDIENCE PUT STRAWBERRY SHORTCAKE ON TOP!
WHAT?! IMPOSSIBLE, SHE COULDN'T HAVE CAUGHT UP TO MY LEAD.

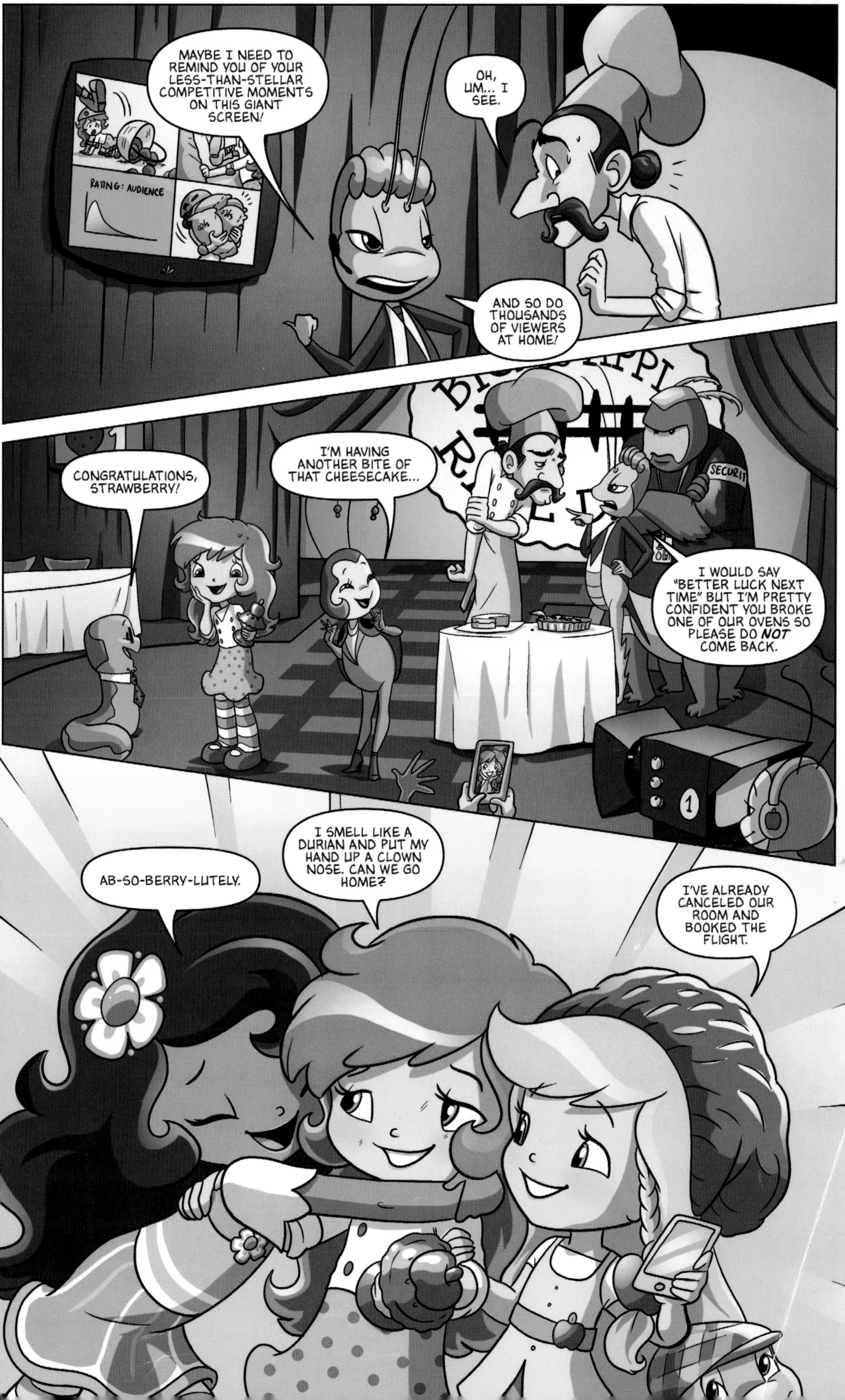
MAYBE I NEED TO REMIND YOU OF YOUR LESS-THAN-STELLAR COMPETITIVE MOMENTS ON THIS GIANT SCREEN!
RATING: AUDIENCE
OH, UM... I SEE.
AND SO DO THOUSANDS OF VIEWERS AT HOME!
CONGRATULATIONS, STRAWBERRY!
I'M HAVING ANOTHER BITE OF THAT CHEESECAKE...
I WOULD SAY "BETTER LUCK NEXT TIME" BUT I'M PRETTY CONFIDENT YOU BROKE ONE OF OUR OVENS SO PLEASE DO NOT COME BACK.
1
AB-SO-BERRY-LUTELY.
I SMELL LIKE A DURIAN AND PUT MY HAND UP A CLOWN NOSE. CAN WE GO HOME?
I'VE ALREADY CANCELED OUR ROOM AND BOOKED THE FLIGHT.

BACK AT THE BERRYKIN NURSERY...

I THINK I'LL SPEND THE NEXT THREE MONTHS IN THIS CHAIR. WHO VOLUNTEERS TO BRING ME FOOD AND WATER?

I WOULD BUT I'M NOT MOVING EITHER.

STRAWBERRY! I SAW YOU ON THE BIG APPLE COMPETITION SHOW, YOU WERE *OUTSTANDING.*

CHUG CHUG

CHUG CHUG

THANK YOU!

AND I JUST WANT YOU TO KNOW THAT I TRIED THE PURPLE PIE-MAN'S NEW BAKERY AND YOUR FOOD IS FAR SUPERIOR.

NEW BAKERY? WHAT NEW BAKERY?

THE NEW BAKERY ON PORCUPINE PEAK, OF COURSE! WELL, GOTTA RUN.

COMPETITION IS GOOD FOR BUSINESS, RIGHT?

RIGHT...

"BESIDES...

"...HOW MUCH TROUBLE CAN HE REALLY CAUSE?"

ESPRESSO YOURSELF

PP

we acce competiti coupon

karma Jar

End.

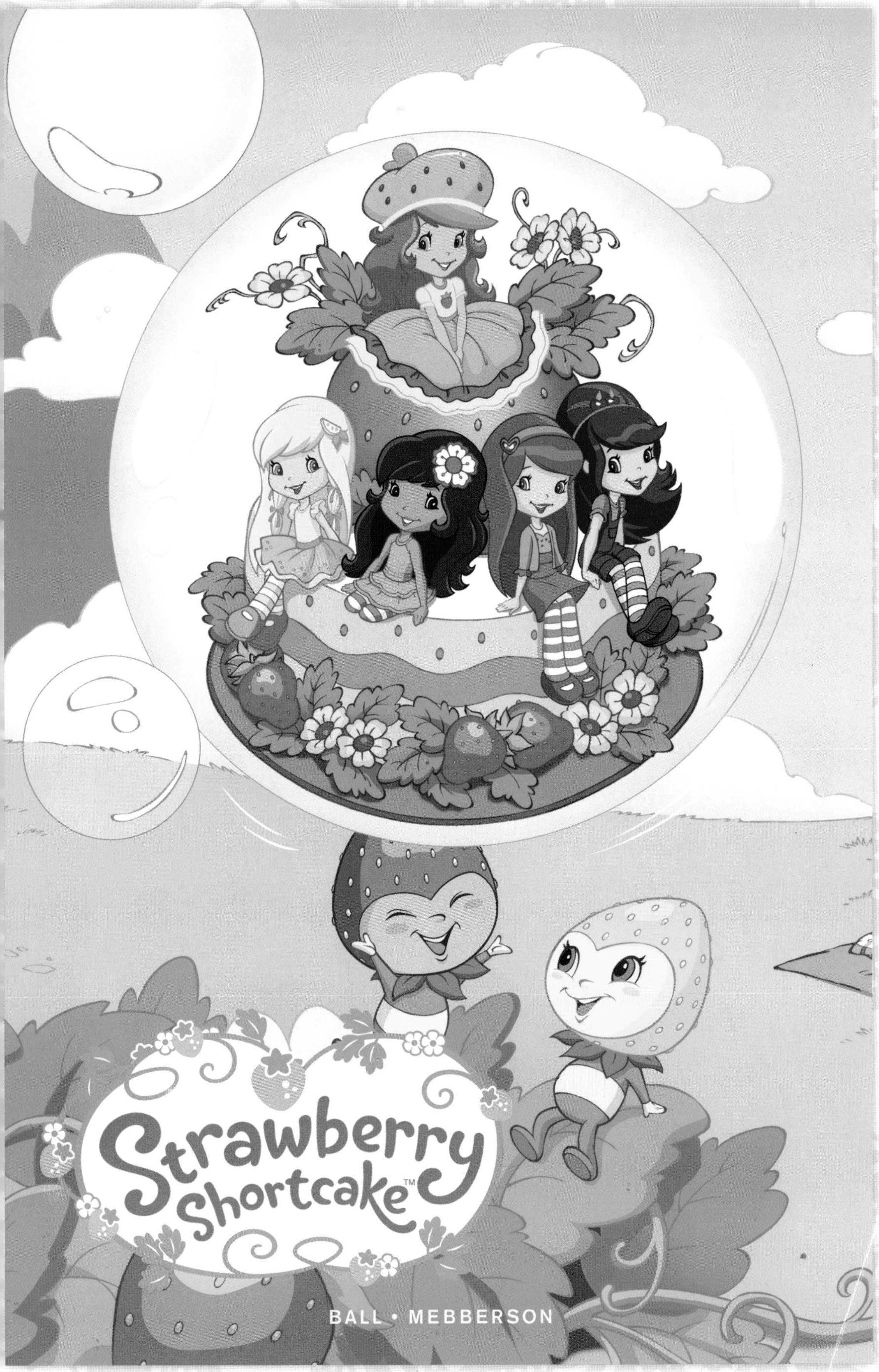
Strawberry Shortcake™
BALL • MEBBERSON

STRAWBERRY SHORTCAKE ISSUE #2, SUB COVER
art by Tina Francisco and colors by Mae Hao

COLLECT THEM ALL!

Set of 6 Hardcover Books ISBN: 978-1-5321-4028-0

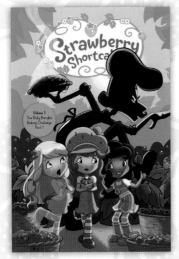

Hardcover Book ISBN
978-1-5321-4029-7

Hardcover Book ISBN
978-1-5321-4030-3

Hardcover Book ISBN
978-1-5321-4031-0

Hardcover Book ISBN
978-1-5321-4032-7

Hardcover Book ISBN
978-1-5321-4033-4

Hardcover Book ISBN
978-1-5321-4034-1